Go, Go, Pogo!

T0337098

Written by Emily Hooton
Illustrated by Jan Smith

Collins

Who is in this story?

Listen and say 🎧 ①

Mum

Download the audio at www.collins.co.uk/839801

Dad

Maz

Pogo

🎧 Maz has got a cat.
Her name is Pogo.

Maz walks to school.
Pogo runs.

Maz walks to her house.

Where is Pogo, Mum?

Pogo is in a box.

tap tap

8

Pogo likes her food.

Pogo is on the bus.

Maz is sad. Where is Pogo?

Maz and Amy play on the boat.

Pogo is home. She wants her food.

Pogo is in the car.
She is not happy.

Pogo does not want her food.
She looks at the door.

Eat your food, Pogo.

Maz is sad. Pogo is not here.

Maz gets a bike. Dad gets a bike.

Let's find Pogo!

Go, go Maz! Go, go Dad!

Maz and Dad are at the park.
Maz sees a woman.

Look! Pogo has got four kittens!

Picture dictionary
Listen and repeat

bike

boat

bus

car

park

run

walk

1 Look and order the story

2 Listen and say

Collins

Published by Collins
An imprint of HarperCollins*Publishers*
Westerhill Road
Bishopbriggs
Glasgow
G64 2QT

HarperCollins*Publishers*
Macken House, 39/40 Mayor Street Upper,
Dublin 1
DO1 C9W8
Ireland

William Collins' dream of knowledge for all began with the publication of his first book in 1819.

A self-educated mill worker, he not only enriched millions of lives, but also founded a flourishing publishing house. Today, staying true to this spirit, Collins books are packed with inspiration, innovation and practical expertise. They place you at the centre of a world of possibility and give you exactly what you need to explore it.

© HarperCollins*Publishers* Limited 2020

10 9 8 7 6 5 4 3

ISBN 978-0-00-839801-9

Collins® and COBUILD® are registered trademarks of HarperCollins*Publishers* Limited

www.collins.co.uk/elt

British Library Cataloguing in Publication Data

A catalogue record for this publication is available from the British Library.

Author: Emily Hooton
Illustrator: Jan Smith (Beehive)
Series editor: Rebecca Adlard
Publishing manager: Lisa Todd
Product managers: Jennifer Hall and Caroline Green
In-house editor: Alma Puts Keren
Project manager: Emily Hooton
Editor: Emma Wilkinson
Proofreaders: Natalie Murray and Michael Lamb
Cover designer: Kevin Robbins
Typesetter: 2Hoots Publishing Services Ltd
Audio produced by id audio, London
Reading guide author: Emma Wilkinson
Production controller: Rachel Weaver
Printed and bound in the UK by Pureprint

MIX
Paper | Supporting responsible forestry
FSC
www.fsc.org
FSC™ C007454

This book contains FSC™ certified paper and other controlled sources to ensure responsible forest management.

For more information visit: www.harpercollins.co.uk/green

Download the audio for this book and a reading guide for parents and teachers at www.collins.co.uk/839801